GIRLS SURVIVE

Published by Stone Arch Books, an imprint of Capstone.
1710 Roe Crest Drive, North Mankato, Minnesota 56003
capstonepub.com

Copyright © 2024 by Capstone. All rights reserved. No part of this publication may be reproduced in whole or in part, or stored in a retrieval system, or transmitted in any form or by any means, electronic, mechanical, photocopying, recording, or otherwise, without written permission of the publisher.

Library of Congress Cataloging-in-Publication Data is available on the
Library of Congress website.
ISBN: 9781669014614 (hardcover)
ISBN: 9781669014577 (paperback)
ISBN: 9781669014584 (ebook PDF)

Summary: With Hurricane Katrina on track to hit New Orleans, twelve-year-old Claudia and her family are preparing to weather the storm. But nothing can prepare them for the awful flooding that occurs when the levees that surround the city fail. Even worse, after a chaotic helicopter evacuation, Claudia and her younger sister become separated from the rest of their family. Now it is up to Claudia to protect and comfort her sister through the tragedy.

Designer: Dina Her

Design Elements:
Shutterstock: Slice Lemon (wave pattern) design element throughout,
Spalnic (paper texture) background throughout

Printed and bound in China. 5783

CLAUDIA
IN THE STORM

A Hurricane Katrina Survival Story

by Denise Walter McConduit
illustrated by Francesca Ficorilli

STONE ARCH BOOKS
a capstone imprint

CHAPTER ONE

Ninth Ward, New Orleans
Claudia's Home
August 28, 2005
4:30 p.m.

Momma had to work, so everything that had to get done around this house was up to me. If I complained she would simply say, "Claudia, we've got to eat, so I have to work."

It wouldn't be so bad if it were only me, but the twins, who are two years younger than me, get away with murder. Zoe and Zack are nine, and one thing I learned about twins was that everyone, except me, thought they were special. So special, they didn't have to lift a finger around here.

I took a basket of laundry out of the dryer to fold and put in another load. Momma was getting off from work early and expected these clothes washed and put away.

After my chores, I went out on the porch and watched my neighbors board up their windows. Hurricane Katrina was brewing in the Gulf of Mexico, even though the sky was bright and sunny. The Weather Channel warned that the storm was making a bull's-eye toward New Orleans.

"Are you leaving for the hurricane?" asked Taylor from across the street.

My friend Taylor is a year older than me, taller than me, and prettier than me. But we're both going into sixth grade; it's just the way our birthdays fell. We walk to school together every day, since we live right across the street from each other. I was glad to live so close to a good friend.

"No, my grandfather just had surgery," I

answered. "Besides, my momma's car needs work before she can put it on the road."

I lied. The truth is that Momma's tires were as bald as four eagles, and she's afraid to drive it out of the Ninth Ward.

"Where are you guys headed?" I asked.

"To Houston by my aunt's house. My daddy said Hurricane Katrina is ramping up to be really bad. Sorry to hear about your Poppa," said Taylor.

"I have an uncle in Houston but—"

Before I could finish my sentence, the twins came barreling out of the house. They're both noisy, but Zoe works on my nerves. Zack is nothing like her. He knows how to stay on my good side.

Zack jumped off the porch to play football with his friend Marcus. They're going into fourth grade.

"Claudia, who's going to Houston?" asked Zoe, Little Miss Know-It-All. "We have an Uncle Charlie who lives in Houston," she continued.

"She already knows, so butt out," I snapped.

"Momma said for you to braid my hair," demanded Zoe.

She had a brush, comb, and tiny black rubber bands in a plastic container.

"Momma said for you to oil my scalp too," she added. "Can you part it zigzag?"

"See you later, Claudia," said Taylor as she went to help her mother carry groceries to the car.

"Why can't *we* go to Houston?" Zoe whined.

I parted her long, thick, wavy hair. "Stop saying you want to go to Houston. You're going to make Momma feel bad." I popped her in the head with the brush. She knew not to mess with me, but I made sure no one was looking.

"Ouch! I'm going to tell Momma," she protested.

"You barely felt that lick on your wild, curly hair," I said. "It's as thick as a lion's mane."

My hair was so short I could only comb it into

two ponytail puffs. It never grew. I don't know where Zoe got her hair or her height from. She's as tall as me and I'm almost five feet tall.

In my heart I wished we could go to Houston too. But Momma was a waitress and worked such odd hours, we never got a chance to leave New Orleans. After high school, Uncle Charlie got a football scholarship to Texas Southern University. Once he left New Orleans, he rarely came back. He fell in love with the big city.

"Ouch, Claudia, you know I'm tender-headed," moaned Zoe.

"And dramatic," I replied.

"Well, I know all about hurricanes because I learned that in school . . . Category 1 to 5."

Sometimes my sister's a fact-spitting machine, constantly showing off what she learned.

"You don't get it. Even if we wanted to, we can't leave because of Poppa's surgery," I told her.

"But I heard Momma on the phone with Uncle Charlie and he wants us to come." Zoe pouted.

After I finished combing her hair, we went inside, and the weather was plastered on all of the stations. Poppa leaned back in his recliner flipping through the channels. "I've never evacuated from a hurricane in my life," he told the TV.

"This house on Andry Street is one of the strongest in the neighborhood. I built it with my own hands, it can withstand a storm." He looked at me and Zoe as if to reassure us.

It was hard to imagine our small dingy yellow house ever being new. The paint had faded to a dusky beige, and many of the wooden railings were missing or broken.

Poppa went on, "This house made it through Hurricane Betsy, and this house will make it through Katrina."

"But my teacher said that parts of the city did flood during Betsy," said Little Miss Know-It-All.

Poppa just rolled his eyes. "It's not going to happen again." His voice was stern and convincing.

"I'll be fine as long as I have 'Sassy' with me," he patted the instrument case next to his chair. *Sassy* was the nickname for his horn. When he was young, Poppa played the saxophone whenever he could. He grew up with Fats Domino, a famous blues singer, and once played in his band.

Momma came home during the latest storm update. She plopped down on the sofa.

The mayor was grim-faced. "It's time for everyone to evacuate now if you can. Katrina looks like it will be a Category 4 hurricane. The Superdome will only be used as a shelter of last resort. Leave now or have a plan in place if you decide to stay. I'm urging all residents to leave now."

We sat quiet in the living room as the words vibrated through the house. Momma glanced at Poppa and bit her lip. She looked like his little girl again. "Think we're good?" she asked.

"Most certainly," said Poppa. "And last night you made a big pot of gumbo, right? We're great! When are we going to eat?"

Still, I could see the worry on Momma's face.

That evening I set the big white bowls and spoons on the table. I cut the loaf of French bread into thick slices and buttered them. The rich dark roux of Momma's gumbo filé was warm and delicious. The flavored stew-like soup was loaded with plump crabs, shrimp, and spicy hot sausage. It was served over fluffy white rice, and somehow, something inside made me feel that everything was going to be okay.

"I know we don't have much, but we always go to bed with a full belly," said Momma.

"Let's bow our heads and be thankful," said Poppa. "Heavenly Father, bless this food and help it nourish our bodies. Protect us from all harm during this hurricane season. We ask this in your Holy Name. Amen."

We ate and chatted about how good the gumbo was. Momma was exceptionally proud because Poppa declared that it was as good as the gumbo he ate at Mrs. Dooky Chase's restaurant.

"May I have another bowl?" asked Zoe.

"Sure," said Momma rising from the table.

"I can get it myself," said Zoe, who was closer to the stove. She got up with bowl in hand and reached for the ladle.

"It's too hot—" cried Momma too late.

Zoe's bowl went crashing to the floor, and the gumbo was splattered across the kitchen.

CHAPTER TWO

Ninth Ward, New Orleans
Claudia's Home
August 28, 2005
6:00 p.m.

"Zoe, how many times have I told you about acting impulsively?" asked Momma. "You could've burned yourself on that hot stove. Now get the mop and clean this up." Momma despised a messy kitchen, and she hated wasting good food.

"Yes ma'am," Zoe replied with tears brimming in her big brown eyes. I almost felt sorry for her because Little Miss Perfect seldom gets fussed at.

Later that evening, we heard a commotion across the street.

"The Harrises are back!" said Zoe.

We ran outside to see what happened.

"The traffic was so bad, I turned around," said Mr. Harris to Poppa. "And I heard there's a gas shortage and cars are being stranded alongside the interstate. It's just too risky," he shrugged.

"Let's just pray that the storm will turn away from New Orleans," sighed Mrs. Harris. "And I certainly don't wish it on the Gulf Coast, I have many relatives who live there too."

"If you need anything, we have lots of water," said Poppa. "We're going to ride it out here."

"Thanks, we should have left earlier, but I was cutting yards all day and just didn't pay attention to the storm," Mr. Harris said.

He cut grass for a living and his lawn is manicured better than nails at the Queen Nails shop. Their small white house with navy shutters is the prettiest in the neighborhood. Drivers slow down just to admire it.

Mrs. Harris works in a daycare and watched the twins when they were little so Momma could work. She's also an African dance instructor and performs on Sundays at Congo Square in the French Quarter. She still refers to the twins as her "babies."

Like I said, everyone loves twins.

"Welcome back," said Momma. "You guys came just in time for a bowl of gumbo. Claudia, set some more bowls out."

"Yes ma'am," I replied. Even though I had just washed the dishes and helped Zoe clean the kitchen floor, I didn't mind. In a way, I was glad to see Taylor and her family. At least I'd have someone to hang out with after the storm.

We all sat together again at the kitchen table while they ate.

"Pops, were you in the neighborhood for Hurricane Betsy?" asked Mr. Harris. "Wasn't it a Category 5 storm?"

"Yes, I was here," Poppa answered. "It hit on September 9, 1965. If I remember right, it was a Category 4. Terrible storm. It wouldn't have been so bad if they wouldn't have blown up the levees to flood the Lower Ninth Ward."

"Now Pops, do you really believe the rumors that they blew up the levees?" asked Mr. Harris. "I personally find that rumor hard to believe."

"I don't trust the government one bit," said Poppa. "The Corps of Engineers claimed that the storm surge from Lake Pontchartrain was so bad, it caused the levees to breach. We took about eight feet of water, and parts of our neighboring parish of St. Bernard took about eleven feet. But I don't have any facts to support the claim. I pray it was just a rumor."

"One positive result of Hurricane Betsy is that the Corps created a 'Hurricane Protection Plan' designed to create a better levee protection for the city," said Mr. Harris.

"I guess we can't escape the flooding though," said Mrs. Harris. "New Orleans is shaped like a bowl, nestled right in between two bodies of water, Lake Pontchartrain and the Mississippi River. Because we're below sea level, we depend on an extensive levee system to protect us from flooding."

"So New Orleans is made like a bowl of cereal?" asked Zoe. "Like Cheerios?"

"Or like a bowl of your momma's good gumbo," Mrs. Harris smiled and winked at Momma.

"Yes, just like that," said Momma. "It's because most of our city is below sea level and surrounded by water. Sometimes if it rains, we have flooding. Or if the storms blow in water from the Gulf of Mexico we can flood."

"But the levees are our first line of defense to keep the water surge away from us," said Mr. Harris trying to reassure us.

"In the 1700s when the Spanish colonists came

to New Orleans, it flooded so frequently they implemented the above-ground burial system," said Momma.

"Why did they do that?" asked Taylor.

"Because when it rained, dead bodies were popping out of the ground." She laughed. "Now tourists come from all over to see our above-ground cemeteries."

"Oh, bodies were coming out like this," said Zack.

He did an imitation of dead bodies popping up. He ran around the kitchen jumping up and down, fingers in his ears, eyes bulging out.

"You're so funny. You look like a zombie!" Taylor squealed.

We laughed as his little scarecrow-like body jumped up and down around the kitchen.

"Taylor, come to my room," I said. "I'd like to show you some of my drawings."

Ever since I took an art class in the third grade, I was into drawing faces. To me, everyone's eyes had a story to tell.

"Claudia, you're such a good artist. Can you draw me?" asked Taylor.

"I could try, but I don't know if I'm that good," I replied.

"Oh yes," gushed Zoe. "She can draw anyone. You should see her picture of Oprah Winfrey!"

Zoe is always so extra, I thought. *What if Taylor doesn't like what I draw? Will she still be friends with me?*

Taylor and I went to my room. My daybed is on one side of the room. Momma bought me a paisley purple bedspread with matching pillows. Across from me were black metal bunk beds for the twins.

"What's this drawing of?" asked Taylor as she looked at the artwork above my bed.

"It's a picture of Zoe when I styled her hair like a unicorn." I smiled.

Zoe was into unicorns for a while. Everything she wore had to have unicorns or she'd pout and have a fit. One day she made me so angry for tattling, I braided her hair like a unicorn for school. Yep, one big plait on the very, very top of her head, tight and stiff. I thought it was funny until Momma saw it and made me take it out. I drew a picture of her anyway.

Taylor sat on the edge of my bed.

"I've never had my portrait done before," she said. "Is this pose okay?"

"Perfect," I said.

I took my time and outlined Taylor's face in pencil. I drew her almond eyes, nose, and mouth. Then, I drew her short curly hair. She had a wide headband and no bangs, so it was easy.

Zoe came in the room and peeked over my

shoulder. "No, it doesn't look like her. You made her nose too big."

I erased the nose and redrew it. Zoe shook her head and sucked her teeth. "Now her eyes are too small," she commented.

Taylor perked up. "How is it coming?" she asked. I could tell that she was worried.

"Well . . . *now* you look like Michael Jackson in 'Thriller'," laughed Zoe.

"Can I see it?" asked Taylor.

"Nope, it didn't come out right," I said. Zoe made me so upset I ripped up the drawing into little pieces.

"We'll try it again when we don't have comments from the peanut gallery," I said pointing to Zoe. "I promise, I'll do another one and it'll be better."

I could see the disappointment in her eyes. "Sure," she said, getting up to leave. "I'm sad you tore up my picture, I really wanted to see it."

"Trust me," said Zoe. "It looked nothing like you. I'm just being honest." She shrugged her shoulders.

How could I explain to Taylor that I really wanted to do a great job on her portrait? She meant the world to me because she is one of the nicest friends I have.

By bedtime, I was tired and frustrated about everything—the storm, Zoe, and my friendship with Taylor.

CHAPTER THREE

Ninth Ward, New Orleans
Claudia's Home
August 28, 2005
9:30 p.m.

Poppa used to say, "If you're going to worry, don't pray; and if you're going to pray, don't worry." I tried to pray about the pending storm but couldn't concentrate. Before bed, Momma made us say a rosary to Our Lady of Prompt Succor, a Catholic Saint who's supposed to protect people from hurricanes.

I think Zoe was worried about the hurricane too because when she's nervous she talks a lot. She was shooting questions about the storm at Momma like bullets before she finally fell asleep.

I closed my eyes but could still hear the winds howling and rain beating in torrents on the windowpanes. Then, I dreamed that our house shifted and was picked up like in *The Wizard of Oz*.

I woke up and glanced over at Zoe. She was sleeping like a kitten. But Zack was gone. He must've crept to sleep in Poppa's bed. They were buddies, and Zack was worried about him since the surgery.

I closed my eyes again and felt like I was drifting to the bottom of the deep blue sea. In my dream I saw a mermaid swirling around me with bright red hair, but she had Taylor's brown face. The creature was smiling at me, and she held something in her hand, a seashell, I think.

Outside, gale-force winds whistled, and I could sense that the hurricane was close. The bedroom windows rattled like teeth on a cold winter's night. I glanced up, but my deep slumber wouldn't allow me to fully open my eyes. Instead, I drifted back under the sea.

I tried to draw the beautiful mermaid in my dreams. But this time she had Zoe's long, thick wavy hair; and in her hand, she carried a unicorn. I tossed the drawing into the sea, and my restless sleep continued.

When I heard soft footsteps come into the bedroom, I bolted upright in bed. Momma whispered, "Shh, Claudia, the power is out. I just wanted to put a lantern in your room."

"Is everything going to be okay?" I asked. The house rattled again.

"I hope so," she said. But when a lightning bolt lit up her face, I saw the fear in her eyes. She kissed my forehead and left the room.

I got out of bed and peeked through the curtains. In the darkness of the waning crescent moon, the trees bent to the rhythm of the wind. Power lines licked the sky, and trash cans rolled down the street like bowling balls.

Across the room, Zoe was snoring while hugging her newest stuffed unicorn. I pushed her to the wall and climbed next to her, hoping the warmth of her body would settle my nerves. She rolled over and draped her arm around my waist.

Spooning with Zoe helped me relax, and by the time I woke up again at around 5:30, it was almost daybreak. The room was drenched in the color of dark purple clouds, and I heard quiet voices talking in the kitchen. I stretched, exhausted from the sounds of last night. Momma and Poppa were whispering as if someone had just died.

"I think the worst is over," said Poppa, looking toward the window.

"I hope so. Sounded like the roof blew off last night," replied Momma. "The whole city is without power."

"I know, but at least we still have gas to cook with," said Poppa.

I tiptoed into the kitchen. "Good morning," I said.

Poppa barely made eye contact. He was staring out into space, deep in thought.

"Good morning," said Momma. "How are you feeling? You were so restless last night."

"The house was shaking, and I heard a *BOOM*." My voice was louder than expected and broke the stillness of the kitchen.

"It was probably a transformer that blew out," said Poppa.

"Claudia, get dressed, I need you to go outside with me to check on the house," said Momma.

While I was dressing, I thought, *what would this woman do without me? I'm her best friend, daughter, helper, and everything else rolled into one.*

I threw on some jean overalls, a T-shirt, and flip-flops and went outside while her precious twins slept like babies.

Poppa stood in the doorway looking outside.

"It's bad but I think we dodged a bullet." He sighed.

The wreckage from the storm was massive. Downed trees were strewn all over the neighborhood, and branches covered cars like blankets. Our car was crushed under a huge trunk, and the railings around our porch had blown clean away. One of the columns supporting the roof laid horizontal on the walkway.

Across the street, my heart jumped at the sight of the Harrises' house. The front right corner of the roof was blown off exposing the wooden rafters to the morning sky.

"Wow!" said Momma. "I wonder if they know part of their roof is missing?"

Roofing shingles scattered their lawn like black paper plates, and their crepe myrtle trees had fallen as if kissing the ground.

"Maybe we should tell them," I said.

"Don't cross the street. It's dangerous. There may be live wires in all this debris. I'll phone them," Momma said with a sigh.

We went inside while Momma tried to call the Harrises on her cell phone. The call wouldn't go through.

The twins got up around 7:30 and were eating their favorite breakfast: white powered donuts and chocolate milk.

"Look at this mess," I said. "Powdered sugar everywhere!"

"We're going to clean it up," said Zoe.

Zack pointed to her hair and put his finger on his lips for me to shush. I could hardly hold in my laughter. The powdered sugar covered the back of her hair like a blanket of snow. While she ate, Zack and I joined in the fun, blowing sugar in her hair.

"I know what you guys are doing, and it's not funny," cried Zoe.

We were laughing so hard we didn't hear Momma come into the kitchen.

"What in the world's going on in here?" She rolled her eyes, but her eyes were laughing too.

"This is not the time for mischief," she added. "We've got a lot of work to do around here. Now all of you, go to your room, get dressed, and Claudia, comb that stuff out of your sister's hair."

After Momma left, we had a donut fight blowing powdered sugar on each other. Zack insisted that since we were already in trouble, why not have some fun? I'll always remember the joy we had that morning, the three of us running around in the kitchen, playing.

After everything was cleaned up, the twins got dressed and settled in our bedroom. Zoe brought out her container of hair supplies. She sat on the floor, legs crisscrossed, while I tugged and brushed out her thick, long locks.

"Can you make two French braids?" she asked.

"Nope, that'll take too long," I said. "What about two twists?"

"Like Princess Leia in *Star Wars*?" she asked.

Before I could answer, she cried, "Claudia, why is the floor getting wet? Where's this water coming from? Water is coming into our room!"

I stepped down on the floor, and braced myself, the cool water was rising up my legs.

CHAPTER FOUR

Ninth Ward, New Orleans
Claudia's Home
August 29, 2005
8:00 a.m.

Momma and Poppa were already in the doorway.

"The levees broke," said Poppa.

Zoe jumped up and looked out the window, her uncombed hair flying all over the place.

"Geez, I'm scared! The whole neighborhood looks like a lake."

"A barge drifted through the levee breach and broke off part of the concrete wall," said Momma. "The water is rising so fast we may have to leave."

We made our way through the water to the front door.

"The water's coming in too quick and there's a lot of debris underneath. We could drown trying to walk through the water," said Poppa.

Despite the rapid surge, we still saw an exodus of neighbors trying to wade through the rising murky slop. Some carried trash bags on their heads or oversized floating plastic containers with babies and toddlers clinging to the insides. Parents were holding on to anything that floated, with children hoisted on their shoulders. Some people carried elderly relatives.

"Hey, Pops, y'all better get out now. The levees broke. Water's getting higher by the minute," yelled Mr. Brown, who lived the next street over. "We're trying to make it to the bridge."

"Just be careful out there," yelled Poppa.

Momma looked at her father. They both knew

that leaving was not an option because of Poppa's recent surgery. Across the street, Mr. Harris was on his roof, surveying the damage caused by the storm.

"Well, let's go inside and get to work," said Momma. "Let's see what we can save so that the water won't ruin everything." She never questioned life. She just did what needed to be done.

"Momma, how high do you think the water will get?" asked Zack.

"I don't know," she answered, "but it's got to stop sooner or later."

Momma and I scrambled through the house putting shoes, clothes, food, baby pictures, and family photos on the tops of chests of drawers and closet shelves. The twins tried to lift everything in our bedroom to the top of the bunkbed, but lots of things still floated freely.

We were frantic running from room to room, but

the water rose to the point that we couldn't keep up. Still we kept going like machines without thinking about where we were, our faces frozen in exhaustion and fear. Poppa opened the front door to let in a breeze, but by then the water was deep in the house.

"Maybe we should make our way to the Martin Luther King elementary school." He sighed. "That building is two stories tall."

"No way. It's an eight-block walk," said Momma. "We'll drown before we make it."

At some point, the twins and I stood on kitchen chairs moving items to keep them from going under. The smell was unbearable. The trash can from the kitchen was floating and circling around and around in the putrid water.

"It stinks in here," whined Zoe. "And I'm hungry."

Poppa put his head down. "You're right, Zoe."

He looked Momma in the eyes as if they had a secret code.

"We have to get up to the attic *now*!" he shouted. "Bring up as much food and water as fast as you can. Anything else that you want to save, bring that too."

Momma's lips were tight the whole time. She'd fought back tears all morning, but when Poppa said to go up to the attic, it was like the levees broke all over again and this time tears rushed down her cheeks.

In the hallway, Poppa struggled to pull out the attic stairs. "Quick, bring whatever you want up here."

Momma held back her tears and sprang into action. "Let's get food, the ice chest, radio, sheets, quilts, and towels. I know everyone is tired, but we have to work fast."

We worked in unison grabbing what we could.

By then, the water was up to our necks, so we walked along the tops of furniture. Finally, we made our way to the attic. Poppa was the last one to climb up. He was carrying a large knife in one hand and a meat cleaver in the other when he reached the top.

"Is anything going to happen to us?" asked Zoe. "I'm scared. I don't want to sleep up here."

"We might need to use this to cut open the roof if the water doesn't go down. God won't let anything happen to us," said Poppa. "We're going to get through this."

The air in the attic felt like an electric blanket turned to the highest setting.

"It's so hot in here, I feel like I can't breathe," I said. Sweat was seeping out of every pore in my body.

Earlier this morning, the attic was the last place I thought I'd be. I never dreamt that by lunch my entire house would be underwater.

"I hope we have enough food and water to last a few days," said Momma. "I'm praying that the water will go down by tomorrow."

Our attic floor, for the most part, was covered in plywood. We stored our Christmas decorations up there, and clear containers with gold and silver tinsel brightened up the dinginess of the space. On one end, tucked between two candles and a penguin, a life-size plastic snowman smiled happily as if welcoming us to his home.

Zack helped Poppa scoot some boxes onto the open floorboards atop old beige insulation. They made room for our supplies: linens, towels, and a blue bucket that would serve as a toilet. The pitch of the roof made parts of the ceiling low. But that was no problem for us since we are not tall people.

From the corner of my eye, I could tell that Poppa was restless and nervous.

"Poppa, you got your medicine, right?" I asked.

"Yes, I have that," he snapped. He seemed contrary about something.

"What is it, Poppa?" asked Zack. "You look worried."

"It's my horn, Sassy," Poppa said. "I think I left it on the top shelf of my closet."

"I'll go and get it," said Momma.

"No, it's getting too dangerous," he replied. "The water is almost to the ceiling. I can't risk losing you."

Before Poppa could stop her, Momma was down the attic steps, her head just above the water. It was the first time I saw my grandfather shed a tear. His eyes were moist, and I saw him wipe away a tear using his jazz-themed T-shirt. We listened and held our breaths as momma waded through the murky liquid.

"I got it," she yelled after what seemed like an eternity.

We sighed collectively and hugged Poppa. We knew how much his saxophone meant to him. He played it in second-line parades, Mardi Gras, and at Christmas parties. It was his constant companion after he lost his second wife, Grandma Mildred.

We heard a commotion in the water, and then, a bloodcurdling scream.

CHAPTER FIVE

Ninth Ward, New Orleans
Claudia's Home
August 29, 2005
Monday evening

I climbed down the steps and saw momma's head bobbing up and down in the water, holding up the instrument case. The side of her face was splattered in blood.

"Quick, Zoe, hand me a towel," I said. My heart was pounding. I jumped into the water to meet Momma halfway.

"I'm okay," yelled Momma. "I cut my forehead on a light fixture, but I'm not hurt. I screamed because I saw a dead rat floating in the water."

Together, we made our way back to the attic stairs.

"Thank you," said Poppa, clutching the case. "I never should've opened up the front door. No telling what other critters are in that water."

Just the thought of a rat had me on edge. Critters love to hide in attics. But after the day's events, I was too tired to dwell on it. We were so hungry, we devoured our sandwiches, chips, and cookies that night. Momma kept trying to call Uncle Charlie on her cell phone to tell him we were safe, but all the lines were out.

By nightfall, we stretched out on blankets, quilts, and pillows. All of us huddled beside Momma like a hive of bees around their queen. It was pitch black except for the golden glow of a few candles. We only used our flashlights when we needed to use the bucket.

A rat didn't stand a chance in the attic with the

way Poppa snored. The twins slept so hard their bodies were like deadweight. I had to roll them off of Momma's arms.

"Claudia, I'm really worried about your grandfather," said Momma in the quiet of night. "He's tired. I can see him slowing down. You are my fearless girl, my little warrior. You're such a gift to this family. Promise me that if anything happens, you'll all look out for each other."

"Of course, Momma," I said. "You know I will."

Momma continued, "When you were born, you were premature, and my mother used to say, 'Don't worry about that little one, she's a fighter, she's strong.' And I must admit my mother was right."

It was a long time since I'd fallen asleep next to Momma. Her smell and the warmth of her body lulled me into a deep, restful sleep. I wasn't afraid of the rat, our house being underwater, or the hurricane.

August 30, 2005
Tuesday morning

The next morning, we had Pop-Tarts and sodas for breakfast. Poppa was busy examining the attic ceiling.

"There's a vent up there, but I can't reach it because the pitch is too steep," he told Momma. "Even if I put Zack on my shoulders, I still couldn't push it out. But it would let in more air."

The morning heat in the attic was sweltering and made us listless. We heard strange noises outside, the sound of water swirling around, voices calling in the distance, weird animal sounds, screams.

"We need to get some ventilation in here," Poppa was looking at the ceiling again. "Here's a good spot."

He pulled out the meat cleaver and started chopping at the wood. The work was long and hard, and after about an hour, he sat down to rest. Momma took a turn hacking at the wood, but a roof has many layers: plywood, black asphalt, and shingles.

Finally, she managed to open up a little hole, and the bright sunlight danced into the room. Poppa, Momma, and I worked all day trying to make the opening bigger and wider using the knife and cleaver. By evening, it was big enough for Poppa to get his fist through.

We all were irritable that day in the smoldering attic. Momma complained that we ate too many snacks. Zack harassed Zoe for whining about being stuck in the attic. Zoe pouted because I refused to spend all day braiding her hair into little braids. Momma certainly didn't have the patience to tackle that head of hair.

The confinement of the attic frayed our nerves and made us restless. Momma listened to the portable radio all day and tried to get help on her cell phone but couldn't. Every hour, we checked the attic steps to see if the water had gone down, but the level didn't budge. By dusk the fear of being trapped in the attic became a reality. We barely ate our peanut butter and jelly sandwiches and water.

"Claudia, you better eat all of your sandwich," teased Zack. "You know rats love peanut butter." He knew that I despised rodents of any kind.

"Maybe I should leave half of my sandwich next to her," Zoe joked. They were teaming up against me. That's one thing I learned about twins; they sure know how to stick together.

By bedtime, the attic was suffocating. No one wanted to sleep near anyone. Zoe sat up in the middle of the night, just staring around the room. Zack constantly got up to check if the water had gone down. Poppa kept peeking out the hole in the ceiling. Momma was just plain worn out from worrying all day. She knew more than what she was telling us about our situation.

I dreamed that I was a soldier in *The Nutcracker* ballet battling rats, but I was losing the fight. Periodically, I'd wake up and scan the perimeter for the slightest signs of movement. Rodents move quicker than the human eye can blink.

But I must've finally fallen in a deep sleep because by morning I heard the sound of a saw. The rhythm was unmistakable, and the voice too.

"Claude, I thought I'd help you guys out," Mr. Harris called out to Poppa from atop the roof.

"Ronnie, you're a sight for sore eyes, how did you get here?" asked Poppa, looking up through the hole in the roof.

"I floated over on a boogie board with my handsaw to help get you and some of our other neighbors out of their attics," Mr. Harris said. "It's bad. The water is not going down, and they're sending in the National Guard. I heard some choppers yesterday. I understand they were rescuing folks stranded on rooftops like us."

"I don't trust no helicopter," said Poppa. "Too many crashes. If I had a choice, I'd rather wait on the Coast Guard. I'm a Navy veteran. But I want to thank you for helping us."

Mr. Harris cut an opening about the size of a washing machine. After he left, Momma and I lifted Zack up on the roof, being careful not to scrape his legs on the jagged opening, then Zack pulled up Zoe. Momma and I had to figure out how to get the rest of us on the roof. We found some old dusty storage containers and stacked them on top of each other for the rest of us to climb up.

Finally, we saw daylight and could breathe in fresh air. We sat bracing ourselves outside on the sloping roof, the sunshine on our faces. The only birds hovering over us were dozens of noisy helicopters.

Looking out on the horizon was a never-ending lake of people on rooftops yelling and waving towels to get the rescuers' attention.

"I want to ride in a helicopter," said Zoe. "I hate living in the attic. Can they fly us to Houston by Uncle Charlie?"

"I don't know where they're going," I replied. "Mr. Harris says they're rescuing people is all I know."

But my sister didn't let anything drop when she wants something. "Look, now there's a copter across the street at Taylor's house." She began jumping up and down. "Maybe they can get us too!" She waved a white T-shirt to get their attention.

"Can we go Momma, please?" she begged.

"Claudia, look, they're dropping a basket to us," she squealed with joy. "I'm getting in!"

Zoe jumped in the basket. The pilot called out, "I've only got room for two."

"Oh no, get out, Zoe!" yelled Momma. "Let's wait and all go together." But the sound of her words was drowned out in the noisy atmosphere.

Momma motioned to me, "Claudia, please go and get her!" I did as Momma asked, but in the split second it took me to jump inside the basket, we were in the air.

CHAPTER SIX

Above New Orleans
August 31, 2005
Wednesday morning

I could hear Momma scream before I saw her crumble on the roof, her words evaporating in the air. Zoe and I rocked like babies in a cradle, back and forth in the silver wired basket. I gazed down below. I couldn't tell my house from any other, the dark-colored rooftops barely visible in the muddy water. People looked like ants waving white flags.

"Whee! Isn't this fun, Claudia?" Zoe smiled as if she were on an amusement park ride.

"No!" I cried. "Momma told you to get out!" I was so angry.

The basket lifted us into the cabin with several other families. I immediately rushed to the cockpit to speak to the pilot.

"Can you go back to get them?" I pleaded, my voice choking.

"Kid, we're just trying to get people off of their rooftops," he answered. "I'm sure someone will get them. There'll be other copters. We're doing this all day long."

His words pierced my heart like a dagger. I sat down next to Zoe, my whole body trembling. I've never been away from Momma, not even to spend the night out. The only time I ever left the neighborhood was for school field trips.

I glanced around the cabin. People looked scared but relieved. An elderly lady kept holding up her arms in prayer, saying, "Thank you, Jesus. Thank you, Lord." I saw some familiar faces but I was so confused that everything was a blur.

Hot tears rolled down my cheeks in deep waves. On one hand I was glad to be rescued from the floodwaters, but at the same time I was worried about what was to become of the rest of my family. *Will they be rescued?* I wondered. *Will Poppa survive this ordeal?*

I held my head down as tears continued to trickle. Someone touched my shoulder, and I looked and saw Mrs. Harris sitting beside me. I turned to her and cried in her arms.

"Don't cry, honey," she said. "We'll make sure to look out for you and your sister."

"Are we going to Houston?" asked Zoe. I just looked at her and burst into tears again.

The ride was quick, less than thirty minutes, then it landed on an elevated section of the interstate. People huddled together in groups, all looking dazed, some with suitcases, trash bags, or any other possessions they managed to bring. Deserted cars were scattered and pushed along the railings. Mrs. Harris shepherded us next to her like little lambs.

"Stay together, children," she said over and over. "Let's just keep together."

"Claudia, you alright?" asked Taylor, squeezing my hand.

"I'm just scared and worried about my family," I said. The kindness in Taylor's eyes told me that she understood.

"Look, Claudia," said Zoe, pointing. "Another helicopter, I bet they're on that one."

The copter landed and we looked at each passenger, but our family wasn't there. Every couple of hours, another helicopter landed, leaving more and more people on the interstate. And with each load, Momma, Poppa, and Zack were missing from the group.

My heart sank hour by hour, and I watched Zoe's giddy mood change to despair. Over time, it was difficult to stay in our cluster. The crowd was getting more frustrated by the minute.

"I need to use the bathroom," Zoe told Mrs. Harris.

"Oh no, my baby," Mrs. Harris said. "I don't know where you can go. There's no place up here."

Zoe began to cry.

"Tell you what, my sweetie, let's just go behind these cars." She took off her African print head wrap and draped it out like a shield so no one could see.

"Just go right here behind this car. You two need to do the same, while it's clear." She took some Kleenex from her backpack. "Use this to wipe."

Taylor and I were embarrassed but grateful.

While we waited, the heat was scorching and tempers were on edge. We were tired, hungry, and thirsty and didn't know where we were spending the night. Someone managed to bring a case of water with them, and a fight began when the water ran out. Some folks brought their animals, and a lady was arguing about not getting any water for her dog. We leaned against the rail to avoid getting crushed by the swelling crowd.

"Look," said Taylor, pointing at a store. "Someone down there in the floodwater is throwing bricks through the window of that store."

"They're probably trying to get water and food. People are desperate," said Mr. Harris. "Just being in that nasty water is dangerous. There could be snakes, lizards, raccoons, frogs, alligators, who knows? But the worst are the red fire ants."

We watched the group kick open the doors and minutes later, run out with diapers, bread, drinks, and cases of water. Then we saw a military truck pull up with soldiers carrying rifles.

Someone in the crowd yelled, "They're only taking the things that they need!"

"Step back," said Mr. Harris. "We don't want to borrow trouble."

Several shots rang out, and all of us ducked for cover. I didn't know what happened, but after that, the mob grew even more restless. I was frightened for my family. Were they desperate for food too?

Zoe was clinging to Mrs. Harris like glue, her eyes wide as saucers. "I want my Momma." She began to cry.

"I know, my baby," Mrs. Harris said to her. "Just you wait. I know she's coming soon. I can't call her because the cell phone towers are out."

Mrs. Harris knew how to settle her down. But I was still so angry with Zoe, I couldn't stand to look at her with that wild hair. She had loosened her ponytail, and I knew Momma would be mad.

We were stranded on the interstate for what seemed like eternity, the crowd growing in the heat each hour. Mr. Harris managed to finagle three bottles of water for us to share, but we still had nothing to eat.

It was late afternoon when a huge military truck and some National Guards rolled up on the ramp. "I heard they're taking us to the Superdome," said Mr. Harris.

"The Superdome?" Zoe's face perked up. "I've never been to the Superdome."

"We just got to stay together, my babies," said Mrs. Harris. "Just keep close together."

The anxious crowd lunged forward to get on the vehicle but backed up when the soldiers started pointing their guns at them.

"Are they going to shoot us, Daddy?" asked Taylor. "Why do they have guns? Did we do something wrong?"

"Let's just step to the back," said Mr. Harris. "I'm sure there'll be another truck. We did nothing wrong." He walked us to the back of the crowd.

It wasn't until three trucks later before we got on board, and it was still packed.

"Let's just hold on to each other," directed Mrs. Harris, locking arms.

We rolled through the foul-smelling water, pools of gasoline shining on the surface. Almost every store that we passed had its door kicked open with steady lines of people desperate to get in. But the saddest sight were stranded dogs trembling on tops of cars and doorsteps, their eyes pleading for mercy.

Hundreds of people were wading in the water with anything that floated. Some had large irregular-shaped parcels balanced on the tops of their heads. Everyone was walking to the Superdome. As we approached the facility, the on-ramp was flooded with folks trying to evacuate the city. As we rode, we looked out at the dark brown floodwaters littered with garbage and floating debris, but there was one sight that sent chills up and down my spine.

CHAPTER SEVEN

New Orleans
En route to the Superdome
August 31, 2005
Wednesday evening

If you've never seen a dead body sprawled facedown in a pool of water, I can tell you, it's not a pretty sight. And what made it worse were the rats surrounding it. Zoe screamed so loud at the sight of the swollen corpse, Mrs. Harris had to put her hands over her eyes to block her view. All of us on that truck were shaken.

"That's somebody's relative!" cried Mrs. Harris. "We need help down here. People are literally dying in these waters."

I could feel my heart racing in fear of something happening to Momma, Poppa, and Zack. I grabbed Zoe and hugged her as hard as I could. I began to pray. *Please God, don't let bad things happen to my family.*

I had promised Momma to look out for Zoe, and now my little sister may be all that I have left in the world. I took out one of my ponytail twists and brushed her hair back with my hands. I gathered it up and put it back into a nice, neat ponytail. Momma didn't like her children looking any kind of way. I held my sister close to me and kissed her forehead. She quieted down and looked up at me.

"I want Momma, Zack, and Poppa," she sobbed.

"I know Zoe, and we're going to find them soon, I hope," I said, kissing her.

"But it's all my fault," she said. "Momma says I don't listen . . . and I didn't listen."

"Maybe not, but you didn't cause the hurricane.

Poppa says some things are out of our control," I reminded her.

She looked up at Mrs. Harris and cried, "I just want to go home."

"I know, my baby, we all do," said Mrs. Harris. "We're going to make it too. We just have to stay together and stay strong."

When I got off the truck, so many thoughts swirled in my head. *Is my family safe? Will I ever see them again?*

Armed National Guards herded people up the ramps of the dome. The news media was there, trying to show the nation how bad things were. Desperate people dropped to their knees pleading for food and water with handmade "HELP" signs. Others lay on the ground weak and dehydrated from the intense heat of the day. In one section was an emergency medical triage center with nurses and doctors tending to the elderly and sick.

The crowd was so thick, people's tempers flared and caused fights to erupt. Infants were crying, and separated children frantically looked for their parents.

"Claudia, do you see Momma?" asked Zoe, scanning the multitude of people.

"No," I said. It was impossible to locate her in this vast sea of faces.

"Let's just keep looking as we walk," said Taylor. "They must be here."

Mrs. Harris insisted we move through the crowd as one unit. The National Guards pointed their guns at people in an effort to control the crowd, but it only made matters worse. There were thousands of people stranded at the Superdome with no electricity, air conditioning, food, or water.

They directed us to go inside the dome. But it was like being thrust inside a hot tin can. The hurricane had peeled off a large section of the roof and the sunlight permeated the opening like a spotlight. We walked in and the smell made my stomach turn. The only places to sit were in the stands.

"If we can't sit together, this won't work," said Mr. Harris after scanning the arena.

We sat on the floor of the aisle; people were tripping over us trying to get to their seats. Families were territorial and had blocked off entire sections of rows for their relatives.

"I think I'm going to be sick," said Taylor. She was perspiring and looked as if she were about to pass out.

"Quick, let's get her to the bathroom," said Mrs. Harris. We held Taylor up while we located a restroom in the hallway.

"Oh!" Mrs. Harris gasped when she saw inside the bathroom. "This is horrible! Let's get her out of here."

Inside the restroom, there were overflowing toilets, broken water faucets, and human waste smeared and scattered across the floor.

Taylor threw up. "I feel so weak," she said.

"Let's go outside to get some fresh air," said Mrs. Harris, rubbing Taylor's back. "She may be dehydrated."

We trailed behind Mr. Harris as he carried Taylor to the nearest exit. An armed guard appeared out of nowhere.

"You're not allowed to exit," he said, pointing his rifle at us.

"But my daughter's sick," said Mr. Harris. "She needs medical attention."

"Well just you, no one else," he answered. "We're trying to keep everyone contained in the stadium until the buses arrive."

Just then Zoe stepped forward. "I'm sick too," she said and fell limp to the floor.

Mrs. Harris picked her up and said, "I guess both our girls need to see a doctor."

Zoe winked at me, and I knew that she was just being dramatic. But the guard relented and allowed us to go outside. He directed us to the triage center.

"It's heat exhaustion," said the nurse after examining Taylor. "She needs fluids and some rest. When was the last time you guys had water?" We couldn't remember.

She gave each of us cheese crackers and a bottle of water. "If you can, you need to take her in the shade."

Mr. Harris located a spot outside of the dome next to a family that he knew. They created a small section and let us squeeze next to them.

"We'd rather be outside in the hot sun than inside the Superdome," the gentleman told Mr. Harris. "It's a darn shame, it's like we don't count in America. The government doesn't care about us. We don't have any water or food, and they're referring to us as 'refugees,' as if we're from another country."

"I agree," said Mr. Harris. "And I heard that the president is visiting the Gulf Coast. He's not even coming here."

"The news reporters are asking where's the Red Cross? They're trying to get the word out to the rest of the country," said the gentleman. "I heard that the guards are shooting at looters. Some of these people are just trying to survive, not all of them are bad apples. Man, our government just don't care about poor people. The Red Cross is nowhere to be found."

When I heard this, I thought about what Poppa said about not trusting the government since Hurricane Betsy. It made me wonder if he was right. We settled down in our small piece of real estate on the perimeter of the dome.

"I'm so sorry, Taylor," I said hugging her. "If it weren't for me and Zoe, you wouldn't have been through all of this."

I began to cry. For some reason I felt responsible for everything. Taylor getting sick, her parents having to look out for us. Zoe and I were a burden.

"No, don't feel that way. I like having you guys with us," said Taylor. "I'm an only child, and I love being with you. It's lonely for me sometimes."

That night we sat upright with our backs against the wall of the dome. The sounds of sirens, helicopters, gunshots, and constant noise of people talking made sleep nearly impossible. But at some point, we must have all managed to doze off, because when we woke up, Zoe was missing.

CHAPTER EIGHT

New Orleans
Superdome
September 1, 2005
Thursday morning

Mr. Harris was the first one to notice and alerted all of us.

"Zoe is gone," he said, shaking us. "She can't be far because the family next to us saw her walking off just a minute ago."

"Oh no," said Mrs. Harris. "She's probably looking for her mother. Let's not panic, she must be close."

My heart sank to the pit of my stomach. Taylor held my hand. I was shaking so hard my eyes were twitching. I was trying not to cry again.

"You two stay together and look on this side, and we'll split up and go to the other side. We'll find her. Don't you worry, Claudia." Mr. Harris was so reassuring. It eased my mind.

Just as we were ready to split up, Zoe walked up.

"Where's everybody going?" she asked.

"Where were you? You had us so scared!" said Mrs. Harris.

"I thought I saw Poppa, and I started running to see if it was him, but I turned back around. I remembered you said that we all have to stay together," said Zoe.

"That's right, my baby. See how awful it would've been if we left looking for you and we weren't here when you returned?" Mrs. Harris hugged Zoe.

Even though I was upset with Zoe for running off, I was proud that she was smart enough to come back. The Harrises didn't need anything else to worry about.

"Zoe, where did you see him? I'll walk over and check for you," said Mr. Harris. "Meanwhile, you guys stay put. I'll also take a look and try to find us something to eat. I heard they're getting in some MREs, those military meals, soon."

"Anything will be better than those cheese crackers," said Mrs. Harris.

We remained in our spot for fear of losing our place. A lady next to us offered us a fruit cup. Her family walked three miles in the floodwaters and managed to carry a few bags of food with them. We all agreed that Taylor should eat it.

When Mr. Harris returned, he was excited. He had five MREs—ready-to-eat meals—and bottled water. "Claudia and Zoe, I got news about your family," he said. "I ran into one of the guys from our neighborhood, and he told me they were safe."

"Where are they? I want to see them!" Zoe was excited.

My heart raced with joy. I couldn't believe what I was hearing. "Are they here?" I asked. "Maybe Zoe did see Poppa after all."

"Not exactly," said Mr. Harris. "They were evacuated by boat, either by the Coast Guard or a group called the Cajun Navy, who are rescue volunteers from Lafayette, Louisiana. I believe they got picked up yesterday."

It broke my heart to think that they had to stay in the hot attic for another day. But I was relieved because I knew that Momma made sure that she had food and water in the attic.

"Can we go walk around and look for them?" asked Zoe.

"Not right now," said Mr. Harris. "I was told that they were sent to the New Orleans Convention Center."

"Where's that?" asked Taylor.

"It's about a mile from here, but there's no way we can get there. The city is still flooded," he said.

"I really want to see Momma," said Zoe. Her voice sounded tired and she choked back her tears.

"I promise you both that we're going to do our best to reunite you with your family. But for now, let's eat," said Mr. Harris.

"You two have word that your family is safe, but imagine your poor mother. She must be worried sick about you," said Mrs. Harris.

I thought about what Mrs. Harris said. Momma had already been through a lot and worked hard to provide for our family. Sometimes she worked extra shifts or catering jobs for extra money.

Now with this hurricane, where will we live? Where will she work, and will Poppa be able to still get his medicine from the VA hospital? What about our school? Will we have a school to go to? Just thinking about all of this made me feel sad for Momma.

We sat down to eat. It was our first meal in three days, and it consisted of mac and cheese, crackers, sausage, and a cookie. It wasn't the best, but we were grateful.

A family next to us began picking up their things to leave. They had heard that buses were on the way to transport evacuees to Houston.

"The sooner you guys go to the loading area, the quicker you can get on the bus. They're only telling a few people at a time to avoid a stampede," they said to Mr. Harris.

We scrambled to the area where the buses were picking up passengers and waited on the garage ramp. A long line had already formed and there was confusion about whether or not people were allowed to bring pets on board.

A white lady carried her dog, Snowy, in her arms, and she was in tears.

"They won't let me take her on the bus," she complained to Mrs. Harris. "She's all the family I have. I'm Patricia."

"Maybe I can reason with them. I can't believe they won't let you take her. She's such a small dog." Mrs. Harris walked over to the guardsman in charge to talk with him.

A few minutes later she was back. "I'm so sorry, Patricia. He said that if anyone saw you bring an animal on the bus, then everyone else would want to," she said, patting the lady on the arm. "I don't know why they're being so strict. We lost our dog Rosco last year, and I can't imagine leaving a pet behind."

"But don't worry," said Mrs. Harris to the grief-stricken lady. "I think I have an idea." She pointed to her backpack.

The line to board the bus extended for miles. We patiently waited for our turn in the queue, and Taylor, Zoe, and I enjoyed playing with Snowy. She was such a lovable dog. We agreed that we would all sit together, and hopefully by the time we boarded, Snowy should be tired enough to fall asleep in Mrs. Harris's backpack.

"We're next to get on," said Mr. Harris. By then my legs were so tired they felt like rubber bands.

"Maybe Momma will be in Houston," said Zoe. "I can't wait to see her."

"Zoe, don't get your hopes up, I heard that some of the people at the Convention Center will be transported to Atlanta," Mr. Harris commented.

I stopped dead in my tracks. "Atlanta, not Houston?" I asked. "Then, I just can't get on this bus." I backed up frozen in panic.

CHAPTER NINE

New Orleans
Superdome
September 1, 2005
Thursday afternoon

Once again, I felt trapped. I was separated from my family, first by helicopter and now by bus. The thought of Momma going in the opposite direction from us was too much.

Mr. Harris looked into my eyes. "Claudia, didn't I promise you and Zoe that I'll see to it that you're back with your family? Please trust me. I will keep my word."

I brushed away my tears and got on the bus for the six-hour journey to Houston.

Boarding the bus was chaotic. People were angry because they weren't allowed to bring all of their belongings. Families pushed their way to sit together. When we finally got on, me and Taylor sat in one row, Mr. Harris and Zoe in another, and Mrs. Harris and her new friend Ms. Patricia in another.

As we pulled out, people banged on the sides of the bus, angry that they didn't have room for them. Inside the bus was loud because people were cheering, they were so happy to be leaving. We were relieved that Snowy slept through all the noise.

"I guess Zoe is excited to finally go to Houston," I said to Taylor. "This is what she wanted to do from the beginning."

"Yes, I'm happy to leave this horrible city behind too," said Taylor. "I hope we never come back."

"Maybe so," I said. "But you're lucky. At least you're with your parents."

I couldn't help but feel jealous even though the Harrises had been very kind to us. I missed Momma, Poppa, and Zack. The hole in my heart grew bigger each time I thought about them.

"I know it must be awful for you to be without the rest of your family. Sometimes I'm so envious of people with siblings. It's always just me. That's why I'm looking forward to Houston. At least I have cousins there. I always wished I had a sister," Taylor confided.

"You can have Zoe." I laughed. "She's a piece of work."

We both smiled.

On the interstate, we were surprised to see the number of downed trees and utility poles. The extent of the storm was bigger than I had imagined. Everywhere we looked we saw destruction from the high winds. Billboards were shattered or blown away.

Cars were stranded on the sides of the roads, and crowds of people gathered trying to figure out where to go. At one point, our driver had to get out to move a large tree branch blocking part of the highway.

Even though these sights reminded us of the storm, we were relieved to be on the road. The farther we got out of the city, the more we exhaled a collective sigh of relief. It's as if the stress of surviving Hurricane Katrina slowly dissolved with every mile we drove away from New Orleans.

Some people burst into tears retelling their ordeal. Others just relaxed in their seats staring out the window. I felt defeated, but I put my trust in God. Poppa always said, "When you think there is no way, God will find a way."

We stopped at a rest area and were glad to use a clean restroom and wash our hands. Rumors were swirling on the bus of killings and drownings, fires and suicides. Someone said that over a thousand people had already died from Katrina. I tried not to think about it.

"We're all safe and that's all that matters," Mrs. Harris reminded us. "Material things don't matter. Things can be replaced, not people."

After our stop, I sat next to Zoe, and I kept hugging her. I realized that my little sister was one of a kind, and I loved her for it. I brushed back her hair and tightened her ponytail.

"Guess, what?" she told me. "I think Momma, Zack, and Poppa will be in Houston."

"Why do you think so?" I asked.

"Because I just know," she said. Typical Zoe, but I hoped she was right.

Zoe's face was plastered to the window of the bus, and she called out the names of the towns that we passed: Laplace, Gonzales, Baton Rouge, Lafayette, Jennings, Beaumont. When she saw the sign for Houston, she was thrilled.

"Claudia, we're almost to Houston," she said.

But I was not looking forward to Houston, especially with Momma, Poppa, and Zack not there. I had no way of contacting Uncle Charlie, and I was worried about where we would end up.

It was almost dark by the time we pulled into the Astrodome parking lot, and we were all tired. Ms. Patricia had someone waiting to pick up her and Snowy. It was a good thing too, because dogs were not allowed in the dome. She thanked all of us for helping get her dog out of the city.

When we walked in the facility it was clean with bright lights and a large Red Cross registration table. Mrs. Harris began to hastily fill out some forms, and the lady asked if we were all together. "Yes, we're all together," Mrs. Harris replied.

"We're here to help you guys," said a nice volunteer. She had concern in her eyes. "If you need anything let us know. We have hot food, shower facilities, and clothes. You are not refugees. You are evacuees."

Mrs. Harris smiled at the lady and said, "Thank you. Yes, we are all Americans."

This dome was nothing like the horrible one we left behind. We were directed to a room filled with clean clothes, shoes, and undergarments all sorted by size. Mrs. Harris helped us find outfits—jogging suits, tennis shoes, and underwear. Then we were guided to the shower facilities with soap, shampoo, and other toiletries. After our showers, volunteers served us a good meal—salad, fried chicken, mashed potatoes, and broccoli.

The place was crowded but orderly. There were cots to sleep on already set up with blankets.

"Claudia, we've contacted my sister, and she's coming to pick us up tomorrow afternoon. You girls are more than welcome to come with us," said Mrs. Harris. "We tried to contact your mother, but we never got an answer. We will keep trying. Somehow, we'll find her."

"Maybe our Uncle Charlie will find us," I said. "He lives here in Houston."

Someone had a television on, and we sat spellbound watching the news. Eighty percent of New Orleans was underwater, and the flooding wasn't subsiding. There were fires everywhere, looting, rescues, images of deserted pets, and people still on rooftops. More people were coming into the Astrodome every hour and Mrs. Harris suggested that we stop watching the news and just relax.

Zoe and I settled down together on the same cot; it was nice to have her near me.

"Zoe, do you think that Momma will find us? What if they really are in Atlanta?" I asked.

"Let's just pray about it and ask God to please send Uncle Charlie to get us," said Zoe.

We prayed to get reunited with our family and

then drifted off into a deep sleep. That night, I dreamed that I was swimming in clear blue water. I was playing with a school of dolphins when a huge wave suddenly scattered us ashore. I ran to get a boat to bring the dolphins back to the sea, but all I could find was a bright yellow school bus.

    I returned, only to find that the dolphins had wings and were flying high above the clouds, almost touching the sun.

    How spectacular! I thought to myself as I watched them soar.

CHAPTER TEN

Houston, Texas
Astrodome
September 2, 2005
Friday morning

The smell of breakfast drifting through the room was so strong, I opened my eyes. The rich dark coffee, crispy bacon, eggs, biscuits, and cinnamon rolls woke me right up. I was hungry and surprised at how many people had swelled into the arena. We got up to use the restroom and brushed our teeth. I started combing Zoe's hair.

"You do a good job styling your sister's hair," said Taylor. "Her hair is so long."

"Thanks, want to help? I'm making two braids today and we can each take a side."

Taylor and I worked together on Zoe's hair. She sat as still as if she were our very own baby doll. I think she enjoyed the attention of us making her over.

"I'm so glad to be with you and Zoe," said Taylor, wrapping her arms around both of us. "I feel like I have two sisters."

"You are our Katrina sister," Zoe said with a smile. "I hope your cousins like us."

"And don't forget, I owe you a portrait," I said.

We sat together at breakfast and took our time to eat. Some Red Cross volunteers gave us care packages, games, toys, and candy.

"Claudia, I think I saw someone who looked just like Zack," said Zoe. "But I didn't run over there to see if it was him. He was pushing someone in a wheelchair."

"I'm so glad you didn't," I said. I couldn't imagine losing my little sister again.

Taylor and I both laughed and mocked Mrs. Harris, "Let's stay together my babies, let's stay together."

"But I could've sworn . . . never mind." She shrugged.

It was almost time for the Harrises and me and Zoe to leave. I dreaded this moment because I worried that if we left, how would Momma find us. But Zoe and I didn't have any other options.

We gathered the few clothes the Red Cross had given us in a plastic bag and prepared to leave.

"Uncle Charlie!" Zoe shouted. Her scream was so high-pitched it pierced the walls of the building. "I knew you would come!"

I stood frozen in my tracks. My uncle ran over to us and hugged us so hard I began to weep.

"I've been looking for you girls," he said.

"I've been checking the Red Cross database every day, but your names weren't on the roster."

"My apologies," said Mrs. Harris. "They were probably checked in under our family."

"The Harrises watched over us, and it was so bad, Uncle Charlie. We saw dead people." Zoe began to cry all over again.

"Don't cry. That's okay," said Uncle Charlie lifting her up in his arms.

"I can't thank you enough," he told Mr. Harris.

"And, Momma, Zack, and Poppa have been sent to Atlanta," I said bawling again.

"No, no, Claudia, they're here," he said. "I came to pick up all of you. They arrived late last night."

When I heard this news, I sobbed so loud the Harrises, Uncle Charlie, and Red Cross volunteers all ran to console me. The past few days I'd tried so hard not to worry, but now I was falling to pieces.

But the soulful rhythm of a saxophone cut

through the sound of my wails. Someone was playing "Just a Closer Walk with Thee," Poppa's favorite hymn.

"That's Sassy, Poppa's saxophone!" yelled Zoe.

We ran toward the sound, and sure enough, they were all here—Momma, Zack, and Poppa in a wheelchair. Zack rushed over to Zoe and hugged her as only a twin could.

"I thought it was you," she said. "I saw you this morning."

Momma kissed my face. "I knew you would be okay," she said through her tears. "You're a survivor, a little fighter. Thanks for keeping your sister safe. I just don't have the words to tell you how proud I am . . . I love you."

"Hey, are you ready for some of your Momma's gumbo?" asked Uncle Charlie. "I'm so happy to have my family here!"

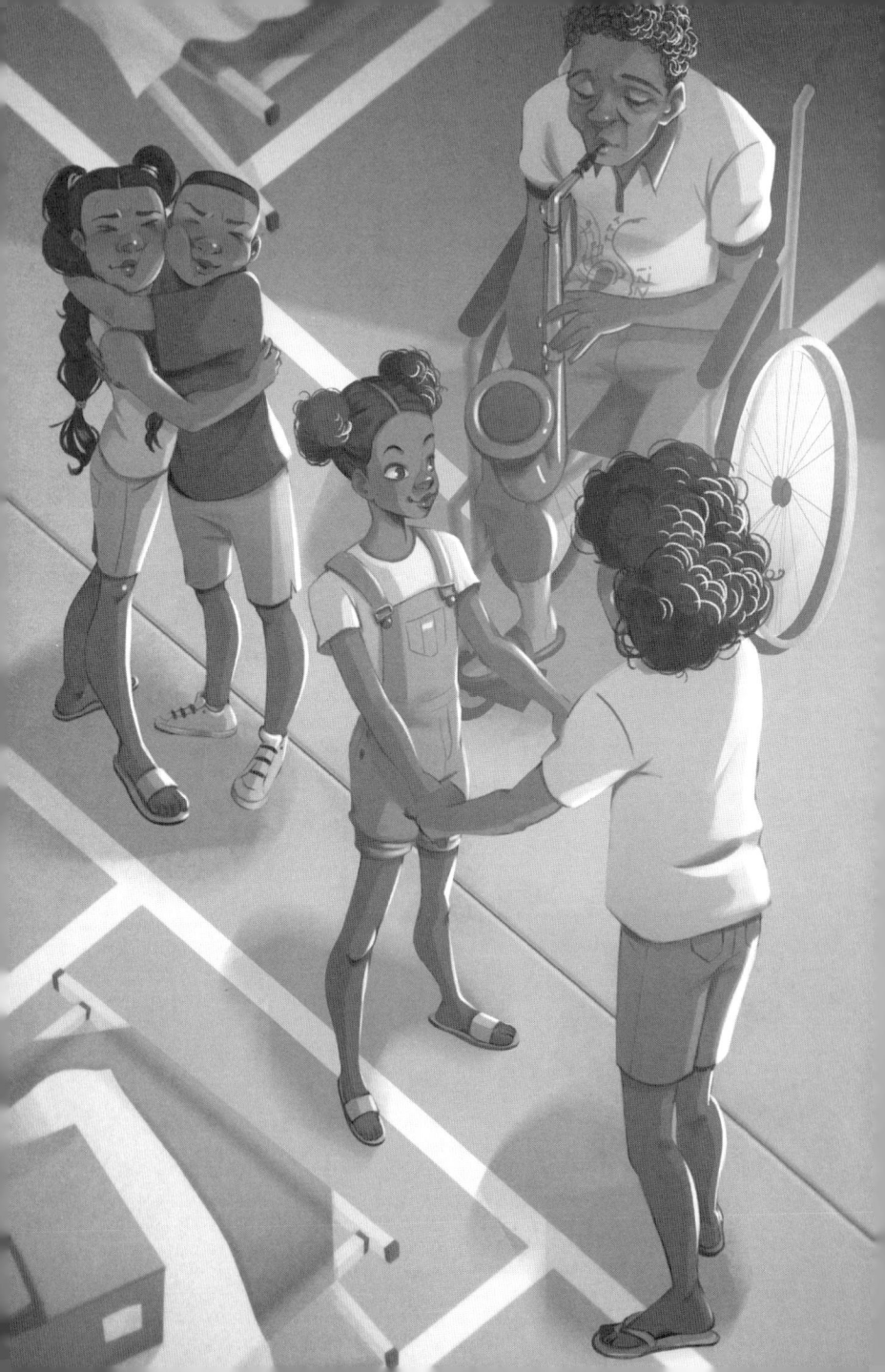

A NOTE FROM THE AUTHOR

Hurricane Katrina barreled slightly east of New Orleans on August 29, 2005, as a Category 4 storm. But the worst disaster in the city resulted from the colossal flooding triggered by an inferior levee system.

In 1965, when Hurricane Betsy flooded most of the Lower Ninth Ward, Congress authorized the United States Army Corps of Engineers to build and design reliable levees. The project was almost complete when Hurricane Katrina hit the region.

The levees, managed by the U. S. Army Corps of Engineers, are created to keep the surrounding lakes and other bodies of water from overflowing into the city. During Katrina, the levees broke in several spots, resulting in major flooding. New Orleans also relies on a secondary pumping system to drain water out and into canals during heavy rains. Sadly, after Hurricane Katrina, the pumps were inoperable.

The people hit the hardest were on the lower social and economic spectrum. Like in the story, there were many reasons people did not evacuate: unreliable transportation, fear of losing pets, illness, or lack of finances.

Writing about Hurricane Katrina and creating a fictionalized version of its effects were personal for me because I grew up in the Lower Ninth Ward and evacuated during Hurricane Betsy. Our house was ruined, and we were forced to temporarily live with relatives.

During Hurricane Katrina, I evacuated to Houston and was stuck on the interstate for 16 hours. What moved me most during my research was the desperation, anger, and frustration people felt during the aftermath of the storm. Due to citywide flooding, they were trapped in houses, stranded on rooftops, holed up in attics, and camped out on porches. Pets were not factored into the the citywide evacuation. Rescue efforts were chaotic, families got separated, people died or were unaccounted for, and communication was nonexistent.

Residents felt a sense of loss, abandonment, and anger toward the government for leaving them without access to food, water, medical supplies, or proper evacuation facilities. The New Orleans Superdome was deemed a "shelter of last resort." It was ill-equipped to handle the 30,000 evacuated residents transported there. The New Orleans Convention Center also lacked adequate supplies to accommodate the number of people brought to that facility.

The American Red Cross did not arrive in New Orleans until weeks after the city was evacuated. The United States, Louisiana state, and local governments failed to develop a coordinated response to evacuate victims in the region. As a result, almost 2,000 people lost their lives because of this catastrophe. Hurricane Katrina displaced an estimated 400,000 residents who went to cities like Atlanta, Dallas, and Houston.

Former New Orleans Mayor Marc Morial commented in his book *The Gumbo Coalition*, "When Lt. Gen. Russell Honoré was assigned commander of the Joint Task Force Katrina responsible for coordinating military relief efforts, the people of New Orleans were living as if they were in the bowels of a slave ship."

The impact of the disaster was massive, sick patients suffered in hospitals that were inoperable, elderly senior citizens were stranded in flooded nursing homes, prisoners were trapped in prison facilities, and the police were overwhelmed.

The initial response in the United States concerning the relief effort was mixed. People in other parts of the country questioned why anyone would live in a hurricane-prone region and were reluctant to help. Some news reporters referred to displaced residents as "refugees" and not "evacuees," which implied that New Orleanians were not real citizens, not real Americans.

Television news channels were instrumental in shining a light on one of the worst disaster responses from the government in American history. They showed desperate people on their knees pleading and begging for help and televised decaying bodies floating in contaminated floodwaters. Critically ill, elderly seniors were pictured cast aside in plain sight without medical care or attention. These heartbreaking images sent shockwaves around the world and moved our nation collectively to have compassion for the victims of Hurricane Katrina.

It was an honor for me to write about this series of tragic events because I lived it firsthand. I used the name Claudia for my main character because I have a friend whose daughter Claudia was so traumatized by her experience in Hurricane Katrina that she still refuses to visit the city. I also cast a set of twins in my story because I know personally that everyone loves twins. I'm from a family of 13 children and we have three sets of twins.

I would like to thank my children, grandchildren, family, and friends who supported and encouraged me during the writing of this book. If you would like to find out more about the hurricane, visit the Katrina National Memorial Foundation Museum at www.knmfno.org or to find out more about the New Orleans levees visit www.levees.org.

GLOSSARY

Corps of Engineers (KOR uhv en-juh-NEERS)—branch of the U.S. Army dedicated to civil and military engineering projects, such as bridges, dams, and levees

debris (duh-BREE)—leftover pieces of something broken or destroyed, as well as animal waste and garbage

dramatic (druh-MAT-ik)—displaying high or extreme emotions

evacuate (i-VA-kyuh-wayt)—to leave a dangerous place to go somewhere safer

exodus (EK-suh-duhs)—the departure of a large number of people

gale-force winds (GAYL-FORS WINDS)—winds of 32 to 63 miles per hour

hurricane (HUR-uh-kane)—a very large storm with high winds and rain; hurricanes are measured on a scale from Categories 1 to 5, with 5 being the worst

impulsively (im-PUHL-siv-lee)—acting without thought or care

levee (LEV-ee)—an embankment built near a body of water to prevent flooding

Lower Ninth Ward (LOH-er NYENTH WAWRD)—a neighborhood in New Orleans

parish (PAIR-ish)—in Louisiana, a section of the state with its own government; a parish is similar to a county in other states

putrid (PYOO-trid)—rotten or full of decay

rosary (ROH-zuh-ree)—a series of prayers often prayed on a special string of beads

saint (SAYNT)—a person who lived an extremely holy life, which is formally recognized by the Christian Church

transformer (trans-FOR-mur)—a device that changes the voltage of an electrical current

MAKING CONNECTIONS

1. Claudia and her family faced multiple challenges during Hurricane Katrina. Discuss the things that went wrong. Were any of the tragedies avoidable?

2. Compare and contrast the conditions at the Superdome in New Orleans with the conditions at the Astrodome in Houston.

3. How did Claudia's feelings toward Zoe change during the story? Why do you think they changed?

ABOUT THE AUTHOR

Children's book author Denise Walter McConduit lives in New Orleans, Louisiana, the birthplace of jazz, a city that enjoys unique traditions like Mardi Gras, jazz festivals, and debutante balls. Preserving cultural traditions through family stories is important to Denise. It's how she grew up and it's what she passes on. Like the stately oak trees that line St. Charles Avenue or the steamboats that dance on the Mighty Mississippi, Denise McConduit is truly a New Orleans treasure.

ABOUT THE ILLUSTRATOR

Francesca Ficorilli was born and lives in Rome, Italy. Francesca knew she wanted to be an artist since she was a child. She was encouraged by her love for animation and her mother's passion for fine arts. After earning a degree in animation, she started working as a freelance animator and illustrator. She finds inspirations for her illustrations in every corner of the world.